Best wishes!
Pete

Gus at Work

by Peter Barbour

This is Gus.

He is a Soft Coated Wheaten Terrier dog. He's happy, friendly, and very
cute.

His owners are Peter and Barbara.

Peter and Barbara took Gus to school to learn how to get along with other dogs and people.

Gus learned how to

sit,

lie down,

and stay.

He was a very good dog.   All things considered, though, he'd rather play.

Soft Coated Wheaten Terrier dogs were originally from Ireland where they lived on farms. They helped keep the farm free of mice, and they helped the farmers herd and guard their sheep.

Peter and Barbara wondered if Gus could herd sheep. They took Gus to

Katherine, at the Blueberry Ridge Sheep Farm and Herding School. Gus

discovered sheep, and he loved to chase them. That was fun, but it wasn't

helpful to the farmer.

Peter and Barbara decided to send Gus to the sheep herding school. Mike,

Katherine's Border Collie dog, often helped her when she worked with Gus.

Mike was very good at herding. When Katherine told him to get sheep, he would run into the pasture, circle the sheep and drive them to her.

When Katherine would shout, "That'll do," Mike would stop herding and immediately return to Katherine's side.

Peter, Barbara, and Gus worked very hard at herding, but it was very hard for Gus to separate work from play. Each day Barbara and Peter would practice with Gus. Far from the sheep, he would follow directions to circle right and circle left. When Barbara would shout, "That'll do," Gus would come running to her.

At Blueberry Ridge, Gus learned how to move sheep out of their pens and chase them down the chutes.

Gus practiced for sheep herding contests with other dogs.

But, what Barbara and Peter really wanted Gus to do was to be able to tend

the flock in the big pasture,

and drive the herd down the path, through the woods, back to the barn.

Gus practiced sitting still in the deep grass as the herd grazed, but he couldn't overcome his desire to have fun. He'd pop up and run at the sheep scattering them all over the field. Barbara would shout, "That'll do." Gus would not listen and continued to play.

When Gus did that, he would be taken from the field. He had to sit far away

from the sheep, in time out, until he was calm.

Gus, Barbara, and Peter continued to practice.

One day, Gus and Barbara were in the pasture, far away from the sheep, when they heard barking and a high pitched, "baa, baa." It sounded like a sheep was in trouble. Barbara could see at the top of the ridge a mother sheep, her lamb, and two strange dogs.

Barbara let Gus off his leash and said, "Gus, get sheep!"

Gus ran to the sheep, and he barked as he ran. The other dogs saw Gus and ran away. The sheep dashed to where Barbara was waiting.

Barbara shouted, "That'll do." Gus immediately returned to her side.

Barbara said, "Sit," and Gus sat. "Good dog," Barbara said and gave Gus a treat. Barbara was very proud of what Gus had done.

When Katherine heard what Gus had done, she was also very proud. Gus continued to practice hard, but every time he got too close to the herd, it was too tempting. He just had to have fun. He'd run into the herd and scatter the sheep all over the field.

One thing he could still do well was scoop the sheep out of their pens and chase them down the chutes. Gus always held his tail high because no matter what he did, he always did his best.

Gus is older now. He no longer herds sheep, but to this day, when Barbara

shouts, "That'll do," Gus always comes running to sit by her side.

"That'll do."

Illustrated by Peter Barbour

Written by Peter Barbour

Photograph by Barbara Barbour

2016

Made in the USA
Middletown, DE
18 October 2016